the pitchers carnation

The Flowers of the Month, Book One

m.k. moore

flirty filth publishing

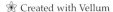 Created with Vellum

blurb

Javier

Pitching was my passion until I met her. I can't get her out of my head or my heart.

Carnie

I don't date players, but he makes me rethink every single thing I've ever thought about the game.

There are no fast-balls or outs here; this safe, short, and steamy novella will leave your Kindle smoking.

This is the first book in the Flowers of the Month series.

one

. . .

Javier

WHEN DID I get this old? I wonder as I sit in an ice bath for the third time this week. I am not old at thirty-two, but my body has had enough. I have put it through a lot, and I have no intentions of slowing down anytime soon. I have been playing baseball since I was five years old. I started in T-Ball and made my way to the big leagues. I have been playing for Atlanta for ten years now. It's home. I grew up in Lawrenceville, so to be able to play for the team I rooted for my whole life has been amazing. My parents are nearby. My little sister is still in college, but she's nearby too. It's nice being a hometown hero, but the national press makes me out to be more than I am. I was dubbed the bad boy of the big leagues fairly early in my career, and it never went away. I don't drink, yet I have had several alleged DUIs. I can't forget about how my steroid addiction is out of control. I've allegedly fathered numerous children. That would damn near impossible, seeing as I've never slept with a woman. My mama would kick my ass from here to Macon if I ever treated a woman like yesterday's boxers.

Early in my professional career, I learned that being that kind of player wouldn't work for me. For some of my teammates, cleat chasers are a way of life, but I avoid them with a ten-foot pole. My job is baseball; luckily, it's my joy too. We are in the off-season right now, and I've had to rest my arm more than usual this year. As a pitcher, it's literally insured for millions of dollars, but my entire body hurts these days. I'm afraid my career is almost over, and I have nothing to fall back on. I went to college, but baseball was my whole life, and I'm not sure what I can do with a liberal arts degree.

"I'll be on vacation for two weeks," Jensen Wilson says, forcing me to open my eyes. He's the team's physical therapist and my best friend. We met on my first day with the team, which happened to be his second day. He's been helping me get my arm back in shape for the season opener in March.

"That's right. Where are you taking your wife again?" I ask. He's married to the team owner's daughter, Stella. They got married about six months ago in the middle of the season, so they couldn't take a honeymoon then. It was a surprisingly simple wedding at an outdoor venue in Trenton, Georgia, near Chattanooga.

"France," he says, smiling. Not for the first time, I wonder what it must be like to be in love.

"Fun," I say. I've only been out of the country a few times, and I didn't have a great time.

"Yeah, anyway, my sister is starting with the team as a masseuse in March, but she'll be on call for PT as she has the training for that as well," he says, but all I heard is sister.

"Your sister?" I ask, raising an eyebrow. I remember her from the wedding. Tiny little thing. Five-foot nothing, thick, juicy curves, and a riot of curly blonde hair. She was in a light pink dress, and she reminded me of a carnation. She looked like she was built for sin. After staring at her for what felt like hours, I walked over to her. She was a stuck-up little thing that all I could think about was burying my cock nine inches deep and making her beg for my seed. Hell, she's all I can still think about months later.

"I don't date baseball players," she said, looking me up and down with disdain. My cock had never been harder. The instant attraction

I felt for her is unlike anything I've ever felt before. Coupled with her bad attitude, I was ready to throw her down and make her mine in front of her entire family. Instead, I decided to play with her a little.

"I don't recall asking you for a date," I replied dryly. I remember thinking all kinds of filthy thoughts about the two of us. I would have asked for way more than a date, but her sass got me right away. Five little words, and I was hooked. I had every intention of asking her brother for her number, but her words next floored me.

"I don't fuck 'em either. Wouldn't want to catch something," she said before flipping her hair and walking away from me. I vividly remember the way it felt when she walked right up to another man and danced with him for the rest of the night. Who the fuck was he? I still wonder about that. Her dirty mouth needed to be taught a lesson, and I'm just the man to teach it, but I didn't have time just then. I've got nothing but time now. Training doesn't start until February.

"Yeah, Carnie. I left her card near your phone. If you need her. See you in two weeks."

"Safe travels, brother," I say instead of what I really want to. No brother wants to hear how badly their friend wants to fuck their little sister. I wouldn't want to, that's for sure.

Out of the tub, I dry off, waiting for my body to warm up on its own. Sitting down on the bench, I reach over, grabbing my phone and Carnie's business card. I text her to meet me at the gym and get dressed without another thought.

Twenty minutes later, I'm walking on the treadmill when I hear the doors open. I look up from my Kindle where I'm reading my favorite James Bond novel, *Live and Let Die.* My heart stutters as I take in her outfit. She's wearing tight black leggings and a multicolored strappy contraption that can only be a sports bra— her hot pink Nike's complete the look.

"You wanted to see me?" she asks.

"Yeah. My arm is killing me. Can you help with that?" It's not a lie, but I could care less about my arm right now.

"Sure. Give me a few and meet me in the PT room."

She looks so flushed. I can't wait to see if that blush creeps down her whole body.

I've been a good man my whole life. I've never taken something for myself, something I haven't earned yet. I want Carnie for myself; I'll worry about earning her later.

two

· · ·

Carnie

DEEP BREATHS, Carnie. Deep breaths. I repeat this over and over in my head as I try, in vain, to calm down. I am about to be all alone with the man who has haunted my dreams for months now. When I met him at my brother's wedding, I wanted him then, but I couldn't bring myself to accept his advances. I read all about him in the media, and I knew I couldn't handle being just another notch in his bedpost. My brother said I had it all wrong, but it was too late. I had to finish school. I really didn't have time for a man, though I often wonder what it would have been like with him. His cocky attitude made me want things I'd never wanted before. The way he's portrayed in the media gave me pause, and instead, I was a royal bitch. I'd be surprised if he wanted anything more to do with me than massage. I kick my shoes off and place them along with my socks in the corner. I like to be comfortable when I'm working, and I hate wearing shoes, so they are always the first thing to go.

I set my room up earlier in the week, and this is the first time I've used it. My brother got me this job and being home in Atlanta is nice after going to college in Boston. I am not only a physical therapist but a massage therapist as well. Pulling my phone out of my pocket, I Bluetooth it to the sound system and play the soothing tones of my Enya playlist. I move around the giant massage table to get a sheet. I sing softly as I smooth it out over the table.

I look up when I hear him clear his throat. He's leaning against the door jam, smiling at me.

"You ready?" I ask, remembering to breathe.

"Yes." He enters the small space, and I am overwhelmed with his scent. It's definitely Irish Spring. He smells clean and fresh without the added junk a cologne offers. I watch as he pulls his shirt over his head and tosses it on the chair in the corner. He steps out of his shoes but thankfully leaves his sweatpants on.

"It's the right arm, correct?" I ask, pumping some massage oil into my hand.

"Yes," he says, swallowing thickly. He sits down on the table but doesn't make any move to lay down.

"You don't want to lie down?"

"For my arm?" he questions, raising an eyebrow at me.

"Okay, we can start there, but I thought I could give you a full workup."

"Full workup?" he asks, cocking his head to the side. Man, he asks a lot of questions.

"A full body massage and I need to practice," I lie easily. I just want to touch him all over. I can totally be professional about it. Can't I?

"Sure. Sounds great," he says, smiling at me. His hair is longer than it was last season, and it falls over his eyes. He looks roguish. My pussy throbs in my tight pants, and I have to bite my lip to keep from moaning out loud.

After rubbing my hands together, I place them on his shoulder and begin to rub the tight muscles. He groans and drops his head back. I work slowly and methodically from shoulder to elbow. After thirty minutes of just working on his arm, I have him lie down on his stomach. Getting more oil, I work the muscles in his back.

"Your muscles are so tight," I murmur, working on a tough knot in the center of his back.

"I've been under a lot of stress lately."

"Oh. Your girlfriend doesn't offer you stress relief?" I ask and then immediately regret it. So unprofessional on so many levels. He chuckles, his body vibrating under my hands.

"I don't have a girlfriend, Carnie. First of all, I'm not a teenager, and secondly, no woman has ever captured my attention."

"Never?"

"Nope. I've been too focused on my career, which doesn't really allow me the chance to meet any quality women."

"I see."

"What about you? Does your boyfriend help you out?" Now, it's my turn to laugh.

"I don't have a boyfriend." Never have had one, but that doesn't matter right now. Touching him feels right. His perfectly tanned, chiseled body under my hands feels right. In order to get my license, I had hundreds of hours of practice, but no one's body has ever felt this good.

"What about the man you danced with at your brother's wedding?" he asks. Is his voice hopeful? I wish I had more experience with men, so I'd know these things.

"Man?" I ask, thinking back that far. " Oh, that was Gordon, my cousin. His husband was overseas for work and couldn't come to the wedding."

"Cousin? I thought you were trying to make me jealous."

"No, not at all."

"It worked," he says softly.

"Why?" I whisper, still rubbing his back.

"You know why Carnie. You had to have felt the pull between us. Even when your words were harsh, your eyes were soft, your face flushed." He turns over and stares up at me. "Just like you're flushed now. Your tight pants leave nothing to the imagination. I can see that your pussy is wet. Tell me it's not wet for me."

"I, uh," I begin, but I am flustered. No one has ever spoken to me like this before. He sits up and grabs my wrists, pulling me closer to him.

"Tell me, Carnie," he demands. Instead of telling him what he already knows, I wrap my arms around his neck and let him kiss me. His tongue dances with mine, and his hands land on my bare back, just above my waist. I don't stop him when he peels my pants down my legs, to my knees. "Let me see your pussy," he growls. Quickly, he stands and lifts me onto the table. Suddenly, my pants are gone, and my legs are spread wide. "So pink and pretty." He reaches out to touch me, his fingers hovering in midair over my clit. He looks up at me, a devilish smile on his gorgeous face.

"I'm not going to stop you, Javier," I whisper, saying his name for the first time.

"Say my name again, Carnie." His voice washes over me, goosebumps spring up on my skin, and I am powerless against him.

"Touch me, Javier. Be the first man ever to touch me." She bites her bottom lip and looks at me with hope.

"I'm the first man to touch you?" he questions.

"Yes," I nod vigorously.

"I'll be the only man to touch you. You're mine now, Carnie. Mine. You belong to me. Tell me you understand."

"I understand, Javier," I reply, nodding again.

Who knew being unprofessional would lead to this?

three

· · ·

Javier

MY FINGERS SHAKE SLIGHTLY as I hold them over her pussy. I can feel the heat coming off of her. I want her more than anything I've ever wanted in my life. Swallowing thickly, I run my fingers through her wet heat. I pull my fingers from her and put them in my mouth. She tastes like sin. Dropping to my knees, I bury my face in her pussy. I drag my tongue from her clit to her ass. She gasps and throws her head back. The New Age music heightens the experience somehow.

"More. Please, touch me more," she begs. I slide two fingers into her and pump them in and out. My cock is barely contained by my suddenly too tight sweatpants.

"I thought you didn't fuck baseball players," I murmur.

"Don't throw my hastily said words at me," she giggles.

"Hastily?" I question, going back to alternating my tongue and my fingers.

"I was flustered. You flustered me," she moans as I continue to pump my fingers in and out of her. I pull my fingers out of her cunt and move up her body with my lips. Her bra zips in the front. Slowly, I unzip it and peel it from her chest. Her tits bounce free, and my mouth waters.

I lower my head and pull her nipple into my mouth. Gently, I suck and bite it before moving on to the other one.

"Fuck," I groan as the taste of her skin intoxicates me. She tastes like vanilla and cinnamon.

"Javier, please. More. I need more."

Freeing my cock, she gasps and reaches for me. "If you do that, this will be over before it even starts," I groan, grabbing her wrist before she has a chance to touch me.

"Oh, sorry."

"Don't be," I say, gripping my cock. She wraps her legs around my hips, and I run my dick through her wet folds before I slowly push into her. She wraps her arms around my neck and pushes herself onto me further. "There's no going back now."

"I don't want to go back," she says, and I push through her cherry. Knowing that I am the only man to ever be with her like this makes me feel like a fucking king. Her king. Her tight pussy grips me, and I lose my mind. I pause, hoping to give her a chance to adjust, but "Don't stop." Her moans spur me on to fuck into her roughly. I know I should be going slowly, but I can't. I literally can't. The table under us creaks and groans as we move faster and faster together.

"Fuck, you're so tight, Carnie." When I woke up this morning, I never imagined that I'd be here like this with her. Months of feverish dreams are coming true at this moment.

"You're so big. I feel so full," she moans. I pull out of her and look down between us. The evidence of her innocence on my cock. I should have made love to her in a nice bed with fucking rose petals, but it's too late now. I slide back into her. "It feels so good."

Over and over again, I slam into her; she meets me thrust for thrust. Reaching between us, I rub her clit until she screams my name. I follow quickly behind her, filling her with my seed. After a few seconds, I pull out of her and rest my forehead on her chest.

"Let's get out of here," I say.

"Where are we going?" she asks, hopping down off of the massage table.

"Let's grab a bite to eat, and then we'll head to my place."

"Sounds good. What did you have in mind?"

"Chinese?"

"Yum," she says, pulling her pants back on. I chuckle as she hops on one foot putting her socks and shoes back on.

After getting dressed, I pull her into my arms, kissing her. I take her hand and lead her out to my car in the parking lot. I help her into the passenger seat, closing the door behind her. I pull out of the parking lot and onto the street, heading toward a nice restaurant near my condo.

"We should have done this months ago," I say.

"Yeah. Sorry I was such a bitch that night."

"You weren't a bitch; I shouldn't have come up to you like that."

"I had just read an article about you in a magazine that said you got some singer pregnant. I didn't want to be just another girl to you."

"I assure you that I've never gotten anyone pregnant before. You're the only woman my cock has ever been inside of."

"What? That can't be true. I can't be upset that you have a past, but don't lie to me," she says, wringing her hands in her lap.

"I'm not lying to you, Carnie. I swear. I never made time for women before. I was too busy with my career to party or do the things the other guys on the team do."

"That was your first time too?"

"It was."

"Maybe we should skip Chinese and just order a pizza," she says, reaching over and grabbing my hand. Her fingers entwine with mine, and I'm pretty sure my heart skips a beat.

"Yeah?"

"Yeah. We should try that in bed, don't you think?"

"Hell yeah," I say, pulling into the underground parking garage of my building. I screech into my parking space. Inside the elevator, we kiss until we reach my floor. My place is right next to the elevator. We are inside, and she's pressed against the door in seconds. I kiss her and lead her to the bathroom. I fill the tub with hot water and help her out her clothes. "I don't have fancy soaps or anything, but I have Dial." I hold up the bottle of liquid gold like I'm their spokesperson or something.

"Dial is fine," she says, laughing. "Why am I taking a bath?"

"You must be achy, and I'll be joining you."

"Ooh, sexy," she says, climbing into the tub.

"Yes, you are," I say, stripping and climbing into the tub behind her.

I wash her body and let her wash mine.

Is it possible to fall in love with someone you barely know yet at the same time know them better than anyone else ever has?

four

. . .

Carnie

THE HOT SOAPY water cascades over his body as I wash him off. His muscles ripple under my touch. I could touch him forever.

"*Dios mío*," he murmurs. "Your hands are fucking magic. I don't know how I'm ever going to let you touch other men." His alpha attitude is hot as hell; even when I know I shouldn't think it is, I can't help it. The look on his face is serious but adorable. I can't help imagining a future together.

"I promise I won't be touching them like this. I won't be touching anyone, but you like this. Even my outfit today was just for you. I'll have to wear scrubs to work."

"Scrubs? That might even be hotter," he groans.

"I assure you that it's not." As soon as I get to his cock, I feel it harden in my hand. It's my turn to play now. I wrap my fist around his cock and pump it.

"Fuck, baby. You don't have to do that," he groans but doesn't stop me.

"I want to," I say before leaning forward and licking the head of his dick. He leans back, and I take more of him down my throat. His hands tangle in my hair. He guides me, but not too roughly. Water splashes out of the tub as I do it. Everything is going to be a mess, but I don't care.

"Fuck, your mouth is so hot, Carnie. Choke on it," he says, pushing my head down more. Why do I like this so much? "I'm going to come; pull off if you don't want me to come down your throat." I suck harder and harder until I feel him come in my mouth. I swallow all of it down and slowly pull off of him. I stand up and climb out of the tub. I grab a towel and dry off as seductively as I can, which, let's be honest, it's a freaking miracle that I didn't fall down. Despite the lack of sexiness, he watches me with attention.

"You coming?" I ask from the doorway. His head is hung back on the edge of the tub; his breathing is ragged. I feel powerful. I did that. I made him feel like that.

"Oh yeah, baby. I just need a minute to be able to feel my legs," he says, making me giggle. I move from the doorway to his big bed and settle myself in the center of it. "You are so fucking gorgeous." His growly voice washes over me, and I can't help squirming in anticipation. For twenty-two years, I avoided men like the plague. I was saving myself for my husband, but one look from Javier and I didn't think twice this time.

The more time I spend with him, the more I feel for him. It's crazy. I have no idea why I'm feeling this way, but I've decided to just go with it. He joins me on the bed. He's on his knees between my parted thighs. When he leans down to kiss me, I wrap my arms around his neck. His lips travel down my neck to my chest. I feel his hard cock nudging against my opening. Moaning, I move my hips a little to take him into me.

"I could do this forever," I moan, then realize what I said. "I mean…"

"Don't take that back. I am pretty sure we established this is forever. There's no going back."

"Oh, good. I don't think I could ever do this with another man."

"Damn right," he says as he fucks into me harder and harder. I move with him, enthralled by everything that's happening between us, no matter how fast it's happening.

He kisses me at the same time, and I lose it. My body shakes as my orgasm overtakes me. I feel him come inside me again. No protection at all. I never wanted children, but the thought that I could have his child makes my heart swell. He pulls out of me and lies down beside me, pulling me closer to him. I snuggle into his chest. A little while later, his breathing has evened out. Like a creeper, I lean up on my elbow and stare at his sleeping form.

Growing up in Atlanta, baseball was huge in my house. I remember when Javier joined the team. I watched him on TV several times a week. I wanted him then, but the stories about him reached my ears. I hated it, but it didn't stop me from wanting him. It's insane how badly I wanted him. What's even more insane is that I'm in the bed of the bad boy of baseball. And I'm the only one who has ever been in it. How freaking cool is that?

"Why are you watching me sleep," he says, breaking out in a big grin.

"I don't know. Mostly, I think I just can't believe that I'm here," I say.

"You're right where you belong," he says, sitting up and resting his back against his headboard. "Let's get to know each other."

"What do you want to know?" I ask.

"Everything."

"Okay. I grew up in Atlanta, went to UGA, and I was Miss Georgia Peach 2020. I like science fiction shows and am the only girl in my D & D guild."

"I play in a local celebrity guild. I'm a co-dungeon master."

"Well, that's a bit wild."

"I'm a baseball-playing nerd. I've never admitted that before."

"That somehow makes you hotter."

"Does it?"

"Oh, yeah."

"Where have you been all my life?"

"I think I was literally right down the street, but I'm like ten years younger than you." I giggle.

"There's that."

We end up talking most of the night, only interrupted when my stomach growls. We order a pizza, pepperoni, and mushroom, both of our favorites, and continue talking. Between talking and making love, we stay up all night.

In the morning, I pull on his t-shirt, leaving a sleeping Javier, and go out into the kitchen. I intend to make breakfast for my man, but when I get out there, I'm startled by an older woman loading groceries into the fridge.

"Oh crap, you scared me," I say, clutching my chest.

"*Dios mío*," she says. "Who are you?"

"I'm Carnie, uh, Javier's friend."

"Friend, huh? I'm his mama."

"Oh my God, Mrs. Hernández. It's so nice to meet you," I say, fiddling with the edge of the t-shirt.

"Please call me Amrita. I've never met one of Javi's girls before. This is weird."

"Um, yes," I say, agreeing with her.

"I do his shopping. That's weird too, isn't it?"

"No. Of course not. It makes sense. He's on the road a lot during the season." She nods, and that seems to be that. She's really nice and not making a big deal about a half-naked girl in her son's kitchen.

"Would you like some coffee?" she asks, going over to the coffee pot. He must have it set to brew at a specific time.

"Yes. Please. I was just going to make Javier some breakfast."

"We can make it together."

We decide on omelets and bacon. That's his go-to breakfast. While the bacon is sizzling away in the pan, he comes into the kitchen wearing a pair of shorts.

"Hey, mama," he says, coming over to me. He kisses me on the cheek. "Good morning, baby," he says. His accent makes me shiver.

"Hello, son. I was just getting to know your delightful friend."

"She's more than a friend, mama. She's going to be my wife."

"Wife?" She and I both say at the same time.

"Yes," he says simply, grabbing a piece of bacon from the pan. He eats it nonchalantly like he didn't just stop the world from spinning.

I'm totally in love with this man, and I'm gonna marry him one day.

five

. . .

Javier

three months later

I'VE BEEN on the road for three weeks straight, and I miss Carnie. City after city, I've had to make do with nightly video chats with her. Currently, I'm in a Las Vegas hotel room. I'm exhausted after a win that didn't take place until after four extra innings. Is it crazy that I don't like hanging out with my team-mates? They are off doing whatever it is that they do when we are on the road. They stopped asking me if I wanted to go with them a long time ago. I could be down in the casino, but gambling my hard-earned money isn't my idea of fun. My fucking arm is killing me. I threw at least 140 pitches today without relief. I know that I can't keep doing this. A hot shower helps, but I need Carnie's magic touch. She doesn't travel with the team, so I pop some ibuprofen and order some room service. A little while later, there's a knock at the door. Opening it, I come face to face with Carnie. I wasn't expecting her but fuck, am I glad to see her. I missed her more than I thought I did.

"Surprise!" she shouts, lunging at me. She clings to me like she hasn't seen me in years instead of mere weeks. I cling to her as well. I really did miss her.

"I was just thinking about you. I love you so much," I say.

"You do? That's the first time you've said that" she says, looking confused.

"It is?" Surely, I've said that before. Thinking back, I realize that I haven't.

"Nope. That was the first time."

"Well, I definitely love you, Carnie. More than I ever thought possible." Despite not knowing her for very long, I can't imagine my life without her.

"I love you too," she says. Leaning down, I kiss her just as the room service gets here. I sign for it and tip the guy, closing the door behind him.

"Want to split my dinner with me?"

"Sure," she says, setting her purse and overnight bag down on the chair. After eating, we end up in bed. After making love to her, I lean my head on her chest, still buried inside of her.

"Marry me, now," I demand, flexing my hips. I'm not above using my cock to get what I want from her.

"Yes," she moans. I grin and fuck her even harder. I'd be surprised if we didn't get a noise complaint as the headboard slams into the wall on every thrust of my hits. Afterward, we get dressed and go down to the hotel's wedding chapel. She's wearing a hot pink knee-length dress and black high heels, and I wear the only suit I brought with me, the one I have to wear when traveling with the team. After a short wedding ceremony, we are married, officiated by a man dressed up as Gandalf.

"My mom is going to be so pissed," she says, looking down at the rings on our fingers once we are back in the room.

"She'll get over it, especially when you tell her that you're pregnant," I say.

"What?" she asks, looking at me like I have two heads. Is it possible that she doesn't know?

"Are you really going to tell me that you're not pregnant?"

"I'm not," she says, then pauses. I watch as she adds up something on her fingers. "Oh shit. I might be."

"Yeah."

"How did you know before I did?" she asks.

"Your belly is a little distended," I say, and she looks at me like I'm insane. "I mean, just a little. And while I don't know much about women, you haven't had a period since we met."

"Well, shit, I thought it was stress. You, the new job." She grabs her purse and moves to the door.

"Where are you going?" I ask.

"The drug store. I'll be right back," she says, kissing me.

"I'll go with you."

"No, you stay here and ice your arm. I'll take care of it when I get back."

"You sure?"

"Yep."

She leaves, and I ice my arm, waiting for her to return. Thirty minutes later, she does, a bag in tow. She throws it down on the chair and digs through it, pulling out a pink and purple box. "Be right back." She hightails it into the bathroom. Briefly, I wonder if I should go in with her, but I decide against it. I love the woman, but there should be some mystery, right?

A few minutes later, she comes back out with the test stick in her hand. She doesn't look happy or sad, so I have no idea what to think.

"Well?" I ask, somewhat impatiently.

"I'm pregnant!" she exclaims. "Are you okay with it? I mean, we've never talked about babies."

"Of course. We've never once used protection. I knew what I was doing," I tell her. She jumps into my arms, and I spin her around. Setting her down on her feet, I kiss her deeply. I've never felt so scared and happy at the same time. Thankfully, my father showed me what a good father should be like. I've got this.

"Well, what do we do now?" she asks.

"Move in with me," I say.

"Well, seeing as we are married, I don't see why I wouldn't." She giggles. "Where do you have to be next?" she asks, rubbing my shoulder, making me groan in relief. Fuck. She knows just how to work my muscles.

"Tucson. We leave tomorrow," I tell her.

"Should I join you there or go home?"

"Join me. We will go back to back to Atlanta on Sunday." I turn and pull her into my arms again.

"Okay, sounds good, husband. We can do an actual honeymoon when the season is over," she says. Kissing her again, I realize that I'm the luckiest man in the world. My sweet carnation is mine forever.

epilogue

. . .

Carnie

one year later

LOOKING DOWN into our son's crib, I realize how much my life has changed for the better in such a short amount of time. He's sleeping, and while I want nothing more than to pick him up and play with him, I can't. If I do that, he'll never go back to sleep. I slip out of the room, closing the door behind me. In the hallway, I run headfirst into Javier.

"You're home!" I exclaim softly. I wrap myself around him. He drops his bags on the floor and lifts me up. He carries me to the bedroom and sets me down on the bed. He strips out of his clothes and peels my robe off of me. "God, I missed you so much," I say though he's only been gone for a few days.

"I missed you too, baby," he growls before sucking my right nipple into his mouth. I moan as he moves down my body. He buries my face in my pussy and takes me to that place where I don't even know my own name. Then he's inside of me, and I wrap my legs around his hips. I meet him thrust for thrust. Over and over, he slams into me until my pussy clenches, and I scream his name.

Afterward, I lay in his arms. "How was the game?" I ask, having missed it. My parents were over for dinner, and we got sidetracked, fussing over the baby.

"We lost, but we have a doubleheader against them tomorrow."

"That sounds arduous."

"It will be, but we'll get them in the end."

"I know you will, baby."

"How was your day?"

"It was good. I'm ready for my maternity leave to be over," I say. I still have two weeks left, but I'm ending it early.

"You are? Can you leave the baby already? I'm having a hard time going to work each day," he says.

"That's not what I meant. That will be hard. Probably the hardest thing I'll ever do but being alone all day is making me crazy. Don't get me wrong, I love Junior, but no rule says I have to stay home forever."

"That's true."

"Our moms are going to alternate watching him. I start back to work tomorrow."

"If that's what you want, of course, I'll support you," he says.

"Thanks," I say.

"I mean it. I didn't mean to belittle the choice. If you want to work, you definitely should."

"I know. It's fine. I love you," I say, rolling over.

"I love you too. I'm sorry."

"You don't have to be."

"But I am," he says. I feel him move behind me, his chest against my back. He kisses my neck.

"All right, I forgive you," I moan. His fingers reach down around my hip and find my wet pussy.

Falling in love with him was easy. So is staying in love with him. My sexy pitcher shows me how much I mean to him every day. The family we've started means everything to me, but I won't survive another day cooped up in this house. I know my limits. Thankfully, he understands mine too. I can't wait to see what the rest of our lives are like.

epilogue

. . .

Javier

ten years later

TEN YEARS and four sons later, I'm retired from baseball. I'm currently the head coach at the local high school now, and I gotta say, being home with Carnie and kids at the end of every day is so rewarding. My team has won the state championship twice in the three years I've been coaching.

"I'm home," I shout, coming into the chaos that is our house. The kids are shouting as per usual. While they don't actually fight, they do everything loudly. Walking into the living room, I see that they are playing some kind of video game. It's loud and obnoxious—something with skateboards. I didn't know skateboards were still popular. Video games were never my thing, and I don't get the fascination with them, but it keeps all the boys occupied for hours at a time.

"Where's mama, Ryan?" I ask my youngest son. He's patiently waiting his turn. He flips through his comic book.

"She's taking a bath or something like that," he says, gesturing to our bedroom.

"Okay. Abuelo is picking you guys in twenty minutes. Shoes

on," I tell them. My dad is taking the boys out to dinner so that I can take Carnie out for our anniversary.

"Yeah, Mama read us the riot act already. We're ready," Junior says, not looking up from his game.

"Alright. Give me hugs. We'll pick you up in the morning," I tell them as they pile around me.

"Bye Dad," Jason says. He's the second oldest, but he might as well be thirty.

"Have a good time with your grandparents," I tell them just as my dad knocks on the door then opens it.

"Abuelo," they shout and are gone before I have a chance to say anything to my dad.

Chuckling, I make my way down the hallway to our bedroom. Carnie is sitting on the edge of the bed, putting lotion on. Fuck, she has gotten more beautiful as the years have gone on. She's still naked from her bath, her hair damp.

"Hey, baby. Happy anniversary," I say, leaning down to kiss her.

"Happy anniversary to you too," she replies, smiling up at me.

"I had the whole night planned, but seeing you like this, makes me want to stay in and order pizza like the first night we were together."

"That sounds nice. Did the boys leave?" she asks, still rubbing lotion on her skin.

"Yeah, just now." She nods, and I grin at her.

"Well, come here, husband," she says, moving backward on the bed until she is in the center of it. Stripping down, I join her.

"I love you," I tell her as I kiss down her body.

"I love you too," she moans.

Life with Carnie has been amazing, and honestly, it's just beginning. We have the rest of our lives together. Every day is better than the last, and I can't see what happens tomorrow.

looking for more flowers?

They are blooming soon. Be sure to check out the rest of the series.

Flowers of The Month Series-Amazon

January The Pitchers Carnation by M.K. Moore
February The Mobster's Violet by Euryia Larsen
March The Lawyers Daffodil by ChaShiree M.
April The President's Daisy by M.K. Moore
May The Mafioso's Lily by ChaShiree M.
June The Hitman's Rose by S.E. Isaac
July The Foreman's Lark by Poppy Parkes
August The Doctor's Poppy by Tamrin Banks
September The Bodyguard's Aster by M.K. Moore
October The Billionaire's Marigold by Kaci Rose
November The Baker's Peony by Alana Winters
December Santa's Holly by CJ Cartwright

acknowledgments

I want to thank my husband, Daryl. You are so supportive of my dreams and I love you so fucking much for like ever.

Thank you, Mama, for all of your support! I love you.

Karlee, thank you for being a friend. #GoldenGirls reference. But seriously, thank you!!!! Love you .6 times!!!

Rachelle, thank you for writing in this world with me! It was so muc fun!!

Elisa, you're the best!

ChaShiree, thank you for being my friend and supporting me, no matter what I write.

JENNY!!! You are the best damn alpha reader a girl could have!

To all of my readers, you guys are the ones that make this possible! Thank you for reading me and taking the time to review. You don't know how much seeing your words of encouragement help me when I am struggling!

XOXO,

MK

other books by mk moore

To Love Series

-Brother in Law to Love

-Heel to Love

-Wife to Love

425 Madison Series **Multi-Author Series**

-Let Me Love You (Book 2)

-Let Me Stay (Book 17) (also A Vitali Crime Family member)

The Ice Cream Shop **Multi-Author Series**

-Love & Candy Canes (Book 29)

Royally Yours

-A Princess for Hans

-A Duke for Carolyne (coming soon)

Love In Norlyn

-Madame President

Regret, South Dakota

-My Aubree

-Her Forever

-My Sheriff

Owned

-Christmas Auction

The Vitali Crime Family

-Don't You Know?

-Don't You See?

-Mobbed Up Love

-So Good

-Xander's Treat

-One Night Wasn't Enough

-Thanksgiving Ever After

-One Night…

-There's No Escaping Him

-Blush For Me

-Revving Her Engine

-Lucky Irish

-Quick To Love

-Kiss Me Forever

-Kiss Me, I'm Irish-ish

Curvy Girl Summer **Multi-Author Series**

-Beach Gotta Have It

Virgin Call Girls **Multi-Author Series**

-Riley's Temptation

7 Deadly Sins **Multi-Author Series**

-Greedy Girl

Spring's Mountain Men **Multi-Author Series**

-Loving A Mountain Man

Oregon Alphas **written with Rachelle Stevensen**

-His Tight End

Silver Fox Series **Multi-Author Series**

-Bachelor No More (Book 2)

-Hunting Gypsy (Book 3)

<u>A Salem Experiment Novella</u> **Multi-Author Series**
-Frankie's Bride

<u>Finding His Love Novella</u> **Multi-Author Series**
-Finding His Heart

<u>Taking The Leap Series</u> **Multi-Author Series**
-A Bad Habit (Book 5)

<u>Hoppily Ever After</u> **Multi-Author Series**
-His Easter Bride (Book 4)

<u>A DILF for Father's Day</u> **Multi-Author Series**
-Make Me A Daddy (Book 3)

<u>Holiday Firecrackers</u> **Multi-Author Series**
-Conrad's Firecracker (Book 8)

<u>Chasing Dreams</u> **Multi-Author Series**
-Fondle My Beard (Book 6)

<u>Tiaras & Treats</u> **Multi-Author Series**
-Shear Love (Book 8)

<u>The Virgin Surrogates</u> **Multi-Author Series**
-Preston's Luck (Book 5)

<u>Hungry Hearts</u> **Multi-Author Series**
-Hungry For Curtis (Book 9)

<u>I Love Mounties</u> **Multi-Author Series**
-Lost

<u>The Holiday Belles</u> **Multi-Author Series**

-The Hitman's Christmas Wish (a Vitali Crime Family Novella)

<u>Flowers of the Month</u> **Multi-Author Series**

-The Pitcher's Carnation (Book 1)

<u>Kissing Junction, TX series</u> written with **KL Fast**

-Candy Corn Kisses

-Thankful Kisses

-Candy Cane Kisses

-Champagne Kisses

-Chocolate Kisses

-Midnight Kisses

-Shamrock Kisses

-Summer Kisses

-Cowboy Kisses

-Justified Kisses

<u>The Gallucci's</u> written with **KL Fast**

-Anthony by KL Fast

-Trinna by MK Moore

<u>The Doll Duet</u> with **KL Fast**

-Cecilia

-Valentine written with **KL Fast**

<u>America's Sweethearts</u> written with **KL Fast**

-Rebel

-Riot

<u>Dancing</u> written with **KL Fast**

-Dancing Into Love

<u>Mister Yum</u> **written with KL Fast**

-Mister Landlord

The Norton Brothers (Box Set) with **KL Fast**
-Top Dog

All for Love Series written with **Elisa Leigh**
-Daddy Captain

The Boss Duet written with **Elisa Leigh**
-Keeping Her Safe (Book 1)

Whelan Brothers written with **Elisa Leigh**
-Lucky in Love by MK Moore
-The Spare Whelan by MK Moore

Forever Safe Summer Series **Multi-Author Series**
-Loving Summer written with **Elisa Leigh**
-Blind Love
-Swearing To Love You written with **ChaShiree M.**
-Curvy and The Beast written with **Elisa Leigh**

Forever Safe Christmas **Multi-Author Series**
-Her Christmas Wish (Book 2)
-Kissing Kringle written with **KL Fast** (Book 10)
-A Queen For Christmas with **Elisa Leigh** (Book 25)

Forever Safe Summer II **Multi-Author Series**
-Wishing On A Sunrise (Book 12) **written with KL Fast**
Forever Safe Christmas II **Multi-Author Series**
-Loving Kringle written with **KL Fast** (Book 16)
-A Moosehead Christmas written with **ChaShiree M** (Book 21)
-Dirty Claus (Book 25)
Forever Safe Christmas 2021: Christmas Village **Multi-Author Series**

-Unholy Knights written with <u>ChaShiree M.</u>

  -Merry & Bright

<u>Holiday Honeys</u> **Multi-Author Series**

-Holiday With A Scrooge **written with KL Fast**

<u>Beach Babies (A Flirt Club Novella)</u> **Multi-Author Series**

-Baby, Don't Go

<u>NSFW</u> **Multi-Author Series**

-My Bangin' Boss **written with KL Fast**

<u>Party at the Tower</u> **Multi-Author Series**

-After The Party (Book 5)

<u>I'm Yours</u> **Multi-Author Series**

-Seducing Doctor Mancini (Book 9)

<u>Falling On The Fourth</u> **Multi-Author Series**

-Red, White & Bang (Book 4)

<u>Thankful For The Jones Sisters</u> **Multi-Author Series**

-Falling For Sue Ellen (Book 4)

<u>Tattooed Bride Series</u> **Multi-Author Series**

-Loved With Color (Book 2)

-Loved By Him (Book 5)

-Loved Forever (Book 7)

<u>Valladares Family Saga</u> **Multi-Author Series**

-Benicio's Dilemma (Book 1)

<u>The Law Trilogy</u> **Multi-Author Series**

Beyond The Law (Series One, Book 6)

-Under The Clerk written with **E.L. Alexander**

Breaking The Law (Series Two, Book 6)

-Model Prisoner written with **E.L. Alexander**

After The Law (Series Three, Book 6)

-Appeal To Me written with **E.L. Alexander**

Moosehead Minnesota Series written with **ChaShiree M.**

-Marry Grinchmas

-Sterling and Kennedy

-A Rose for Max

-The Time Between Us

-A Moosehead Christmas: Hamm & Ava

-A Moosehead Valentine: Sterling & Kennedy

-A Moosehead Spring: Max & Rose

-A Moosehead Summer: Jace & Penny

Queen of Hearts Ink Series written with **ChaShiree M.**

-Inked Heart

-Inked by Him

-Inked by Her

-Ink Me

-Ink My Soul

The Jorgensen's written with **ChaShiree M.**

-Loki

-Bill

-Hailey

-Torran

-Erika

-Hank

-Erik & Lanie

-Sven

about the author

MK is married to the love of her life. She lives in Tennessee with her husband. She is an avid reader and loves telling steamy stories she deems filthy contemporary. She loves meeting readers, so come hang out with her!

FACEBOOK: https://bit.ly/2PlRV6t
Goodreads: https://bit.ly/2G02bSl
TWITTER: https://twitter.com/smutyourmouth
Amazon: https://www.amazon.com/~/e/B0745G4CJ4
BOOKBUB: https://bit.ly/2QgXZCE
TIK TOK: https://www.tiktok.com/@authormkmoore
INSTAGRAM: https://www.instagram.com/mkmoore0320/
Email: mkmoore032010@gmail.com
Newsletter: http://eepurl.com/hbYi0T
For more flirty, filthy fun check out my Facebook group with KL Fast:
https://www.facebook.com/groups/KLMKGPR/